DROUGHT AND PEOPLE

NIKKI BUNDEY

 Carolrhoda Books, Inc. / Minneapolis

First American edition published in 2001 by
Carolrhoda Books, Inc.

All the words that appear in **bold** type are explained in the glossary that starts on page 30.

5b / Bibliothèque de l'Assemblée nationale, Paris / 9b / John Fox Images; Val & Alan Wilkinson—title page / Philip Wolmuth 16 / 11t, 23t / Hutchison Picture Library; Piers Cavendish 4,11b / Ben Edwards 5t / Yann Arthus Bertrand 7 / Marco Siqueira 8 / Caroline Penn 9t / Roger Scruton 13 / Paul Forster 18t / Eliza Armstrong 18b / Javed A Jafferji 19 / Material World 26 / Clive Shirley 28b / Impact Photos; Jorgen Schytte—cover (inset) left, 24b / S Asad—cover (inset) right / Mark Edwards 10, 12b, 28t / Lior Rubin 17b / Adrian Arbib 22 / Kevin Schafer 24t / Thomas Raupach 25 / DERA 27b / Edward Parker 29 / Still Pictures; M Jenkin 6t / J Sweeney 6b / H Rogers 12t, 27t / J Greenberg 14 / Eric Smith 15 / M Beard 17t / M Jellife 20t / B Turner 20b / D Clegg 23b / TRIP.

Illustrations by Artistic License/Genny Haines, Tracy Fennell

Carolrhoda Books, Inc.
A division of Lerner Publishing Group
241 First Avenue North
Minneapolis, MN 55401 U.S.A.

Website address: www.lernerbooks.com

A ZOË BOOK

Copyright © 2001 Zoë Books Limited. Originally produced in 2001 by Zoë Books Limited, Winchester, England

Library of Congress Cataloging-in-Publication Data

Bundey, Nikki, 1948–
    Drought and people / by Nikki Bundey
        p. cm. — (The science of weather)
    Includes index.
        ISBN 1-57505-498-1 (lib. bdg. : alk. paper)
        1. Droughts—Juvenile literature. 2. Weather—Juvenile literature.
    [1. Droughts. 2. Weather.] I. Title. II. Series: Bundey, Nikki, 1948–. The science of weather.
    QC929.25.B857   2001
    363.34'929—dc21   00-009387

Printed in Italy by Grafedit SpA
Bound in the United States of America
1 2 3 4 5 6—OS—06 05 04 03 02 01

CONTENTS

NO CLOUDS IN THE SKY

All living things on earth need warmth, light, and water to stay alive. Without the sun, there would be no plants for food, no animals, and no people. In hot weather, the sun heats up **liquid** water in oceans, lakes, and streams. Some of the water dries up, or **evaporates**. It turns into a **gas** that mixes with the air. The gas is called **water vapor**. The more water vapor the air holds, the hotter and damper we feel. Hot days can also be stuffy and **overcast**.

There are no clouds in the sky, so there will be no rain. People love warmth and sunshine, as long as we can keep cool and don't get too thirsty. When it is too hot and dry, we are uncomfortable.

Droughts can happen in many parts of the world. They are most common in hot, **tropical** countries such as India. Without rain, plants droop and die, and animals go thirsty. People become desperate for water.

We call unusually hot weather a **heat wave**. A long period without rain is called a **drought**. The two situations often go together, but not always. The weather can also be cold and dry, or hot and rainy.

Long heat waves and droughts make life hard. People, plants, and animals may even die.

Long ago, people believed that if the rains did not come, the gods must be angry. Tlaloc was the rain god of ancient Mexico. People danced and made sacrifices to him in times of drought. Modern people know why droughts occur, but we still cannot stop them from taking place.

5

GETTING WARM

Temperature is a measurement of heat or cold. Celsius and Fahrenheit are the most common scales used to measure temperature. The units of measurement are called **degrees**.

Humans are **warm-blooded** creatures. Our brains have **nerve cells** that can control the heat of our bodies. Unlike snakes and lizards, we do not rely on the sun to keep our bodies warm.

The human body works best when its temperature is about 98.6 degrees Fahrenheit. If we get too hot, we might suffer from **heatstroke**. If the body temperature rises above 108 degrees, a person may die.

These instruments record the weather in a desert in the United States. We record temperature with instruments called **thermometers**. Temperatures between 60 and 85 degrees are common in summer.

This tourist has collapsed on the beach on a hot day. The nerve cells that control her body temperature cannot cope with the heat. The best treatment for heatstroke is to cool the body as quickly as possible.

People with pale skin might become red in the face when their bodies overheat. The color is caused by the blood vessels that widen to let out warmth.

Luckily, our bodies can release heat in several ways. The heart pumps warm blood around the body through **blood vessels**. If the body overheats, nerve cells tell the vessels near the surface of the body to widen. Then more heat can pass out through the skin.

GIVE ME WATER!

Humans need water to stay alive. In many parts of the world, drinking water comes directly from a well, a river, or a lake. The food we eat also contains water.

There is water in our blood and in other parts of the body. The body uses water to **digest** food and to get rid of poisons and waste. An adult human body normally contains about 5 gallons of water.

On a hot day, we want to cool down. Cool water can lower our temperature and wash away stickiness, so we feel fresh.

In the desert, drinking water is often a matter of life or death. People cannot survive for more than two or three days without taking in liquid.

The brain also checks how much water the body contains. If we lose one-twentieth of our normal amount of water, we feel thirsty. That is the body's way of telling a person to drink water. If we lose one-fifth of the normal amount of water, we risk our lives.

Water leaves our bodies in **sweat** and **urine**. In very hot, dry conditions we lose more water than usual.

Sweat helps keep our bodies cool. It is like a sprinkler in a garden. Sweat makes our skin and the air around it cooler and moister.

THE SUN AND SKIN

The sun gives out a huge amount of **energy**. Energy reaches the earth in the form of heat and light. One type of light is called ultraviolet. Too much of this ultraviolet light causes sunburn. Sunbathing can dry out the skin and, over many years, can cause serious illness.

We put special cream called sunblock on the face and body on sunny days. It protects the skin from ultraviolet light. Always wear sunblock during sunny weather.

SLIP! SLOP! SLAP!

This girl from Nigeria, in West Africa, has lots of melanin in her skin. It protects her against the sun. People of African descent who live in cold countries still have dark skin.

When people with pale skin lie in the sun, their skin produces extra melanin as a protection. The skin tans, or turns brown.

If we look at human skin under a **microscope**, we can see that skin has different layers. The top layer contains a natural coloring called **melanin**. It protects us from the sun's rays. People whose families originally came from hot, sunny lands have a lot of melanin. It makes their skin brown or black.

DRESSING COOL

We wear shorts and T-shirts when the weather is hot. These clothes let heat escape easily from our bodies. We can wear long sleeves and hats to protect ourselves from sunburn and heatstroke.

Light colors, such as white, push back, or reflect, the rays of the sun. Dark colors take in, or absorb, the warmth of the sun.

This child has a sunshade, or parasol, fitted to her stroller. It gives her shade and protects her from the heat.

The Tuareg people live in the Sahara Desert in North Africa. Their long, loose robes allow air to flow around their bodies, keeping them cool. Long cloths protect their heads from heat and dust.

Wind is usually cooling, so in hot countries, people sometimes wave fans to make a breeze. During a heat wave, we need shade. We can make our own shade by wearing broad-brimmed hats. They keep the sun from hurting our eyes. Sunglasses make it easier for us to see in bright sunlight.

People often wear hats and carry umbrellas in hot lands such as Malaysia.

HOMES IN HOT LANDS

In tropical countries, houses are designed to stay cool. They may have electric fans or **air-conditioning**. Shutters and blinds on the windows and long porches and wide **eaves** provide shade. People plant shady trees around houses and along streets.

In many countries water is scarce. Every drop of precious rainwater is collected in pools or in tanks called cisterns.

This porch provides a barrier from the sun's rays and is open to any cooling breezes.

In Coober Pedy, Australia, opal miners have built underground houses. The houses stay cool, even when it is very hot outside.

Hot, dry weather affects many of the materials that we use to build houses. Metal swells, or **expands**, in the heat. It carries, or **conducts**, heat well, so a tin roof can become very hot. Paint dries out, cracks, and peels. Tar and **asphalt** may melt.

Many insects live in hot countries, and some of these, such as termites and ants, can destroy the timber used in houses.

See for Yourself

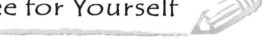

- Place pieces of wood, brick, glass, plastic, and metal outside in the hot sunshine.
- After a few hours, which pieces feel the warmest?
- Which materials are the best conductors of heat?
- Which would make the best building materials in hot lands?

FARMING IN THE HEAT

No crops could grow without the warmth and light of the sun. Plants contain a green substance called **chlorophyll**. This works with sunlight to make the food that keeps plants alive.

Warm sunshine makes seeds start to grow, or **germinate**. It ripens fruit on the trees and grains of wheat in the fields.

Plants need water as well as heat. Hot countries with heavy **rainfall** can produce tropical crops such as bananas.

Drought killed these crops in Zambia, Africa. Without water, crops droop, or wilt, and turn brown. Farmers have developed some grain crops that can survive in dry places.

In some hot, dry areas, farmers move water to crops through pipes or channels. This system is called **irrigation**. Irrigation makes it possible to farm even in the desert. Farmers in the deserts of Israel use plastic to keep moisture from escaping from the soil.

Animals need water to drink, so a long drought may kill cattle. Farmers may have to dig wells to reach water deep underground. Farmers fear very hot, dry weather. It can cause brush fires or turn the soil into worthless dust.

See for Yourself

- Plant two trays with the same kind of seeds.
- Place one tray indoors on a warm, sunny window ledge.
- Put the other tray indoors in a cool, shady place.
- Water both trays equally.
- Which batch of seeds germinates first?

SUN-DRIED FOODS

Hot weather can make food go bad. Bread dries out and goes stale. Milk turns sour, and tomatoes rot and become mushy. The food is spoiled by small living organisms called **bacteria**. Cold stops bacteria from spreading. This is why we use refrigerators to keep food fresh.

Bacteria have made these tomatoes go rotten. They are no longer safe to eat. They would have stayed fresh longer in a cold place.

In many parts of India, people lay out fish to dry in the sun. Dried fish will not go bad, even in the hottest weather. It can be carried away easily to sell in other places.

Sun-drying preserves foods and also toasts or ripens them. These cloves are drying in the hot sun in Zanzibar, Africa.

Some foods are specially dried in warm air or in sunshine. Bacteria cannot grow in these foods, so they are **preserved**. We can eat some of these foods dry. We have to soak other foods with water before we can eat them.

Dried foods such as raisins and apricots are sold in most supermarkets. Sun-dried tomatoes come from Italy, dried mushrooms from China, and dried fish and meats from many parts of Asia and Africa.

See for Yourself

Ask an adult to help you with this project.
Some dried foods can be eaten only after they are soaked or cooked in water.

• Measure two cups of dry rice.

• Pour one cup of rice into a pan of boiling water and let it cook.

• Does the cooked rice take up more space than the dry rice?

• Is the cooked rice softer than the dry rice?
• Which kind of rice would you rather eat?

LONELY LANDS

Many people live in hot, wet places. Very few people live in the world's dry, or arid, zones. Arid regions have hardly any drinking water and are too dry for growing crops or raising cattle. Travel is difficult across the soft sand or the baking rocks of a desert.

Some **nomads** and traders cross African and Asian deserts with their herds of goats and camels. They camp in tents. They travel from one watering place, or **oasis**, to another.

Nomads travel with their camels through the dry lands of northeastern Africa. When the nomads stop to camp, they put up dome-shaped shelters that are covered in mats. The shelters protect people from the hot sun.

A nomad feeds his camel in the desert. There are no trees to shade them from the hot sun.

Oases are fed by wells or underground **springs**. People can grow a few crops there, such as dates, melons, and figs.

Camels have **adapted** to desert life. They can travel on long journeys without water. The fatty humps on their backs give them the energy to go on. Their thick eyelashes keep out the sand.

In some places, water collects underground. People dig wells to tap this water supply.

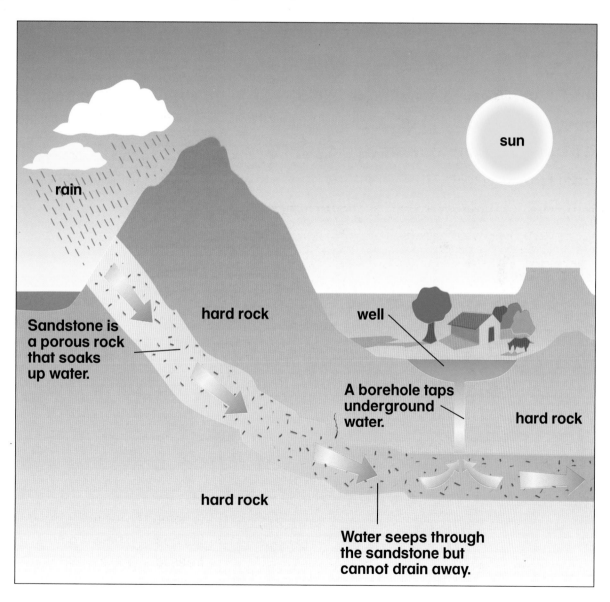

sun

rain

Sandstone is a porous rock that soaks up water.

hard rock

well

A borehole taps underground water.

hard rock

hard rock

Water seeps through the sandstone but cannot drain away.

DESERT EXPEDITION

Deserts are remote places, with few towns. People who go on desert expeditions must carry lots of water. Humans lose water rapidly in the heat. In dry conditions, each person may need to drink between 2 and 7 gallons of water a day.

Travelers use **compasses** to find their way. The compass needle always swings to the north. But it is easy to get lost in sandy deserts. The sand dunes shift with the wind. The shape of the landscape changes, and sand can bury road markers and signs.

Clothes protect the body against heatstroke and sunburn. But travelers need warm clothes, too. Even in hot deserts, nights can be bitterly cold. There are few clouds to trap the earth's heat.

These sheep are suffering from a lack of water during a drought in Australia. The farmer uses a four-wheel-drive vehicle as an ambulance. He will take the sheep to his farm where they can recover.

How would you drive across a hot desert? You would need a **four-wheel-drive** vehicle for extra grip, or **traction**. The tires should be tough, to protect against thorns, but fairly smooth. Too much rubbing, or **friction**, might dig up the sand, so the wheels could get stuck.

Truck drivers try to follow the tracks of other vehicles. Drivers lower the pressure of their tires, so that they hug the ground.

Vehicles often get stuck in soft sand. The drivers have to dig the wheels free with shovels. They push metal racks under the wheels, so that the tires have something to grip.

SUN POWER

The sun gives out power called **solar** energy. We can collect this energy and use it here on earth. A **solar panel** is a flat tile with a black surface that absorbs the heat of the sun. The glass on top helps trap the heat.

Solar panels can heat water or air. An airless space, or **vacuum**, surrounding a tube of water will help keep the water hot.

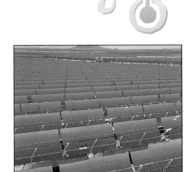

Solar **power stations** produce electricity. The biggest one in the world is in California. Huge mirrors direct the sun's rays onto a giant reflector.

Solar panels are often seen on rooftops in southern Europe, Africa, and Asia. The panels can power hot water and central-heating systems.

Solar-powered vehicles can travel faster than 45 miles an hour. They do not give out fumes that **pollute**, or poison, the air. This car is traveling in Germany.

The vacuum keeps heat from escaping. It **insulates** the water, just like a thermos keeps coffee warm. Solar power is a very **efficient** form of heating.

Small **solar cells** made of **silicon** can turn sunlight into electricity. The cells can power calculators, vehicles, or even spacecraft. Sun power can be used over and over again, unlike gasoline or oil.

See for Yourself

- Fill a large bowl or dishtub with cool water and measure the water's temperature with a thermometer.

- Set the water in the hot sun for two hours. Measure the temperature again.

- Fill a thermos with some of the water from the bowl. Leave the rest of the water in the bowl. Put the bowl and the thermos in a cool, dark place indoors.

- After two hours, measure the temperature of the water in the bowl and in the thermos.
- What is the difference between the two readings?

FORECASTING DROUGHT

All sorts of people need to know whether a heat wave or a drought is on the way. They may be farmers, water company workers, builders, engineers, or travelers.

Scientists called **meteorologists** prepare **weather forecasts**. They study the **atmosphere**, the layer of air that surrounds our planet. The air presses down on the surface of the earth. We measure **air pressure** with instruments called barometers.

These farmers are on their way to the market. Weather forecasters have predicted a very hot day. The farmers travel at sunrise before it gets too hot. The cooler air helps keep their produce fresh.

Low-pressure areas contain rising air. They bring warm, cloudy weather and showers of rain. High-pressure areas contain sinking air. They bring clear, sunny, dry weather, which may be hot or cold. Sometimes great hot and dry **air masses** build up over land, and low-pressure systems cannot move in. This situation produces drought.

This soil has cracked from lack of water. Water for cities and towns is often stored in large pools or tanks called **reservoirs**. During droughts, reservoirs may run dry, putting public health in danger. Water companies may have to limit water use. They might ban the use of water in yards or swimming pools.

Out in space, **satellites** whirl around the earth. They track the movements of high- and low-pressure systems.

FUELING THE HEAT

When we burn fuels such as gasoline, oil, and natural gas, we pollute the earth's atmosphere. Some of the fumes we pump into the air are made more poisonous by sunlight. A thick **smog** can form. People with an illness called **asthma** might have problems breathing.

The gases of the atmosphere are like a blanket around the earth. The gases trap heat around the earth in the same way that a greenhouse traps warmth from the sun.

Smog hangs over Jakarta, Indonesia. The pollution here was caused by forest fires over a vast area of Southeast Asia.

The number of people on earth grows each year, and they all need food. But large areas of the world's farmland are turning into desert.

Air pollution increases the greenhouse effect, creating **global warming** and changes in the world's **climate**. Deserts are spreading, and ice is melting around the **poles**. Some parts of the world are becoming stormier. Heat waves and droughts are becoming more common. If we reduce pollution we can make our planet a healthier—and cooler—place to live.

The sun sets over Mexico City. Here the smog has been caused by pollution from traffic and factories.

GLOSSARY

adapt	To change to survive in particular conditions
air-conditioning	A system that keeps the air in a room or a car cool
air mass	A large, stable amount of air, with roughly the same temperature and degree of moisture throughout
air pressure	The force of the atmosphere pressing down on the earth's surface
asphalt	A black or dark brown substance made from petroleum and often used as pavement
asthma	An illness that causes wheezing, coughing, and difficulty in breathing
atmosphere	The layer of gases surrounding a planet
bacteria	Tiny organisms, some of which can make us sick
blood vessels	Tubes that carry blood around the body
chlorophyll	A green substance inside plants that absorbs sunlight for use in making food
climate	The typical weather in one place over a long period
compass	An instrument used to find direction
conduct	To carry or transmit heat or electricity
degree	A unit of measurement on a thermometer
digest	To break down and absorb food within the body
drought	A long, dry period with little or no rainfall
eave	The edge of a roof overhanging a building
efficient	Doing a job well, with little waste
energy	The power to make something move or work
evaporate	To turn from liquid into gas
expand	To swell and take up more space
four-wheel-drive	Operating with four powered wheels, not just two
friction	The force that slows an object as it rubs against another
gas	An airy substance that fills any space in which it is contained
germinate	To sprout or develop
global warming	The warming of the earth, possibly caused by air pollution
heatstroke	A collapse caused by overheating of the body
heat wave	An unusually long period of hot weather

insulate	To prevent the loss of heat
irrigation	A system for bringing water to crops through pipes or channels
liquid	A fluid substance, such as water
melanin	A coloring, or pigment, found in human skin
meteorologist	A scientist who studies weather conditions
microscope	An instrument that makes tiny objects look larger
nerve cells	Cells that send signals between the brain and other parts of the body
nomad	Someone who has no settled home but moves from place to place
oasis	A fertile area of the desert that is fed by underground water
overcast	Gloomy; blanketed in clouds
poles	The most northerly and southerly points on a planet
pollute	To poison air, land, or water
power station	A building or site where electricity is produced
preserved	Kept fresh
rainfall	The amount of rain recorded in one place over a certain period
reservoir	A lake or large tank created to hold a supply of water
satellite	A spacecraft sent up to circle a planet
silicon	A material found in the earth's crust, used in making solar cells
smog	Fog mixed with smoke or exhaust fumes
solar	Coming from or relating to the sun
solar cell	A silicon chip that converts sunlight into electricity
solar panel	A black plate designed to absorb heat from the sun
spring	An underground stream of water
sweat	Perspiration; moisture given out through the skin
temperature	Warmth or coldness, measured in degrees
thermometer	An instrument used to measure temperature
traction	The grip between two surfaces, such as a tire and the ground
tropical	Describing warm, wet regions near the equator
urine	Waste water passed from the body
vacuum	An airless space
warm-blooded	Having a warm, constant body temperature, regardless of the temperature of the air
water vapor	The gas created when water evaporates
weather forecast	An estimate or prediction about future weather conditions

INDEX